RIDIN

WITH

STYLE

A JUNIOR'S GUIDE TO BMX FREESTYLE

Matt Rider

Contents

Special appreciation to my brother, Ben, for being the inspiration behind this book and for sharing his expertise and enthusiasm for extreme sports. Without his guidance and support, bringing this book series to life would not have been possible. Thank you, Ben, for providing me with the essential tools to turn my dream of writing this series into a reality.

WELCOME TO THE RIDER TEAM

Introduction

WELCOME TO THE THRILLING WORLD OF ACTION SPORTS, where adrenaline meets skill and determination. Meet the Rider Team, a group of friends who share a passion for pushing their limits and pushing the boundaries of what's possible on wheels. Leading the team is Matt Rider, a BMX freestyle prodigy with a style that's as smooth as it is daring. His brother Ben Rider is the team's resident scooter expert, known for his fearless approach to big tricks and bigger gaps. Their cousin, Jack Rider the Extreme Mountain biker, is the team's powerhouse, with strength and stamina that never seem to quit. He's always pushing the limits and coming up with new, innovative tricks. His little brother is Zack "the Ripper", the youngest member of the team, known for his lightning-fast skateboarding skills and his fearless attitude. He's a real crowd-pleaser and has a passion for actions sports that's contagious. And rounding out the team is Rebecca Wheeler, a roller-skater girl with an unshakable attitude and a talent for making every trick look effortless. Together, these five friends are taking the world of extreme sports by storm, and in this series of books, you'll get an inside look at their adventures as they compete, train, and push the limits of what's possible. Get ready for an epic ride with Matt, the BMX pro! In this book he's going to show you all the cool stuff there is to know about BMX Freestyle! He'll even take you to your first skatepark, and when you're ready, your first competition! From the basics of BMX riding, to more advanced tricks and techniques, Matt will be with you every step of the way. I'll let Matt take over for now and guide you through the exciting world of BMX freestyle. So, grab your bike and let's get started!

Hey there! Are you ready to ride the wave of adrenaline and style? My name is Matt Rider, and I'm here to guide you on your journey to mastering the art of BMX freestyle! Whether you're just starting out or looking to take your skills to the next level, I'll be sharing all my tips and tricks to help you ride like a pro. From mastering basic maneuvers to pulling off the sickest stunts, I'll show you how to ride with confidence and style.

But it's not just about the technical side of things, it's all about keeping it fun and promoting the amazing sport of BMX freestyle. So, let's get ready to shred the streets and ride like a champion!

TUCK-NOHANDER

BARSPIN

Chapter 1:
The Evolution

BMX FREESTYLE IS ONE OF THE MOST EXCITING AND DYnamic sports out there. It's a combination of speed, skill, and creativity, and it's no wonder that it's been gaining popularity in recent years.

But did you know that BMX freestyle has recently became an Olympic sport? As a beginner, you may be wondering how you can get involved in this exciting sport. The good news is that it's never too early to start, and with the right training and practice, you too can become a BMX freestyle pro.

In this first chapter, we'll take a look at the basics of BMX freestyle, including the history of the sport, the different disciplines and tricks, and the equipment you'll need to get started.

It all began in the 1970s, when kids started riding BMX bikes on dirt tracks and performing tricks like wheelies and bunny hops. As the sport evolved, riders began to push the limits and develop new and more complex tricks.

This led to the creation of BMX freestyle, which

combines elements of BMX racing with acrobatic tricks and stunts. In the early days of BMX freestyle, riders would perform their tricks in empty swimming pools and at skateparks, but as the sport grew in popularity, competitions began to spring up all over the world. Today, BMX freestyle is a recognized discipline in the world of action sports, and it's even part of the Olympic Games.

But, I'm not just going to teach you how to ride, I'm going to show you the potential of turning your hobby into a professional sport and even an Olympic medal. With the right mindset and dedication, anything is possible. So, grab your bike and let's start riding!

SUPER-WHIP

LOOK AFTER YOUR BMX

Chapter 2:
The Basics

IN THIS CHAPTER, WE'LL TAKE A LOOK AT THE BASICS OF BMX freestyle. We'll cover the different types of BMX bikes, the essential equipment you'll need, and some basic maneuvers that will help you get started.

First, let's talk about the different types of BMX bikes. There are two main types of BMX bikes: race bikes and freestyle bikes. Race bikes are designed for racing on a track. They have a lightweight frame and are built for speed. Freestyle bikes are designed for performing tricks and stunts. They have a stronger frame and are built to withstand the impact of landing tricks.

As a beginner, you'll want to start with a freestyle bike. These bikes are built to handle the impact of landing tricks and are the best choice for learning the basics of BMX freestyle.

Next, let's talk about the essential equipment you'll need. In addition to a BMX bike, you'll need a helmet, gloves, and proper shoes. A helmet is essential for protecting your head from injury, and gloves will help you grip your handlebars and protect your hands. Proper shoes, such as skate shoes, will provide the grip and support for performing tricks. Now that you have your bike and equipment, let's take a look at some basic maneuvers.

The first thing you'll want to learn is the BMX freestyle basic stance. This is the starting position for all tricks and is essential for maintaining balance and control while riding. To get into the basic stance, stand over your bike with one foot on each pedal. Keep your knees slightly bent, and your arms should be relaxed with your hands on the handlebars. The next maneuver you'll want to learn is the bunny hop. This is a basic trick that will help you jump over obstacles and clear small gaps. To perform a bunny hop, ride at a moderate speed, pull up on the handlebars, and lift the front wheel of your bike off the ground. Once you mastered lifting up the frontwheel consistently, the next step is to use your legs to push the rear wheel up and off the ground.

Finally, the last basic maneuver you'll want to learn is the manual. This is a trick that will help you ride on the back wheel of your bike. To perform a manual, ride at

MANUAL

MATTROCOPAN

TURNDOWN

a moderate speed, pull up on the handlebars, and shift your weight backwards. Keep your balance and practice keeping the front wheel off the ground for longer periods of time. These are just a few of the basic maneuvers you'll need to learn to get started with BMX freestyle. With the right training, practice, and attitude, you'll be well on your way to mastering the sport and impressing your friends with your skills.

Remember to always wear the proper safety gear and never attempt tricks that are above your skill level. Always practice in a safe and controlled environment, and have fun!

EURO-TABLE

Chapter 3:
Where to Ride

BMX FREESTYLE IS A VERSATILE SPORT THAT CAN BE PER-formed IN a variety of locations. In this chapter, we'll take a look at some of the different places you can ride BMX free-style, including skateparks, street spots, and competitions.

Skateparks are one of the most popular places to ride BMX freestyle. These parks are designed specifically for BMX, scooter riding, skateboarding, Inline and Roller Skating, and they offer a variety of obstacles such as half pipes, quarter pipes, rails and boxes. They are a great place to practice and learn new tricks in a controlled and safe environment. Many skateparks are free to ride, but some may require a fee or membership.

Street spots are another popular place to ride BMX freestyle. These are locations such as plazas, staircases, and handrails that are found in urban areas. Street riding is all about creativity and finding new spots to ride and challenges yourself. It's important to be aware of your sur-roundings and to obey traffic laws and regulations when riding on the streets.

Competitions are also a great way to showcase your skills and meet other BMX riders. These events are usually organized by local BMX clubs or organizations and can range from small local competitions to large international events. Competing can be a great way to push yourself to improve and to see what you are capable of.

Finally, you can also ride BMX freestyle in your own backyard or driveway. This is a great place to practice basic maneuvers and tricks, and it's a convenient option if you don't have a Skatepark or street spot nearby.

No matter where you choose to ride, it's important to always wear proper safety gear, obey traffic laws and regulations, and to be respectful of the area and the people around you. With so many different places to ride BMX freestyle, the possibilities are endless.

So, grab your bike and get out there and ride!

BUNNY-HOP

TOBOGGAN
AKA T-BOG

Chapter 4:
Skatepark Etiquette

IN THIS CHAPTER, WE'LL TAKE YOU TO YOUR FIRST

skatepark! They are a great place to ride BMX freestyle,

but it's important to be aware of the proper etiquette when

riding there. So first off, we need to look at some of the

basic rules and guidelines, so you can enjoy your time at

the park and ride safely!

The first rule of Skatepark etiquette is to respect

other riders. This means waiting your turn to use the

ramps and obstacles, and not cutting in front of other

riders. It's also important to be aware of your surroundings

and to avoid riding too close to others.

Another important rule of Skatepark etiquette is to obey

the rules of the park. This means following any posted

signs or rules, such as no smoking or no alcohol allowed

in the park. It's also important to be aware of the park's

hours of operation and to ride only when the park is open.

When riding in a Skatepark, it's also important to wear the

proper safety gear, such as a helmet, gloves, knee and

elbow pads, and proper shoes. This will help protect you in

case of a fall and will help you to ride more safely.

It's also important to keep the park clean. This means picking up any trash or debris that you may have brought in with you and disposing of it properly. It's also important to respect the park's property and not to damage any of the ramps or obstacles.

Finally, be aware that many skateparks are also used by other riders such as skaters, scooter riders and in-line skaters. Be respectful of other riders and share the space, wait for your turn and use different obstacles if necessary.

By following these basic rules of Skatepark etiquette, you can help ensure that everyone at the park is safe and that the park remains in good condition. Remember, by following these guidelines, you can help make the Skatepark a fun and enjoyable place for everyone. Happy riding!

SKATEPARK RULES

1. Always wear your safety gear, including a helmet, knee pads and elbow pads to protect yourself from injuries.
2. Watch out for other riders and wait your turn. Avoid cutting in front of others.
3. Avoid overcrowding ramps or obstacles, give others enough space to ride safely.
4. Stick to areas within your level of BMX ability.
5. Ride responsibly by maintaining a controlled speed and avoid reckless riding that could endanger yourself or others.
6. Keep an eye out for newcomers and offer help or guidance if needed.
7. Keep the park clean and dispose of trash in designated bins and avoid littering.
8. Refrain from defacing park structures or engaging in graffiti. Show respect for the park's appearance.
9. Follow Park Rules: Look out for the Skatepark's operating hours and any specific rules or guidelines posted at the facility.

THE SKATEPARK

Chapter 5:
Ramp Types

WHILE WE'RE AT THE SKATEPARK, LET'S HAVE A LOOK around. The majority of a Skatepark is made up of ramps. Ramps are an essential part of BMX freestyle and are used to perform a variety of tricks and maneuvers. In this chapter, we'll take a look at the different types of ramps that you can use for riding BMX, including quarter pipes, half pipes, and box jumps.

Quarter pipes are a type of ramp that is shaped like a quarter of a pipe. They are typically 4-6 feet tall and are used to perform tricks such as airs, grinds, and manuals. Quarter pipes are a great option for beginners because they are relatively small and easy to maneuver. Half pipes are a type of ramp that is shaped like a pipe cut in half. They are typically 6-8 feet tall and are used to perform the same type of tricks but more often in combinations. Half pipes are a more challenging option than quarter pipes and are typically used by intermediate and advanced riders. Box jumps are a type of ramp that is typically used for jumping tricks.

They are usually made of wood or metal and are used to perform tricks such as 360 spins, barspins and tailwhips. Box jumps are a great option for beginners because they are relatively small and easy to maneuver. In addition to these types of ramps, there are also other types of obstacles and features that can be used for BMX freestyle such as rails, ledges, and banks. These obstacles can be used to perform grinds, slides and manuals.

And guess what! Even the walls can be used as obstacles at the skatepark! Wall-ride is a trick where the rider rides parallel to a wall or vertical surface, using the wall as a "ramp" to perform various tricks. Wall-rides can be done on different types of surfaces such as concrete, wood or metal. To perform a wall-ride, the rider will approach the wall at a slight angle, and then lean the bike towards the wall, keeping the pedals level with the wall. The rider will then ride along the wall and jump off at the end, typically back to the ramp or flat surface. Wall-rides can be a fun and challenging trick to learn, and they are a great way to add some variety to your BMX freestyle. It is important to always wear proper protective gear and to practice in a safe and controlled environment.

Hold on tight, because you're in for a wild ride! And the best part is, I've got a surprise for you. I've created a personal **BMX TRICK LIST** just for you! As your riding skills improve, this list will come in handy to help you remember all the sick tricks you'll be pulling off. So what are you waiting for? Flip to the back of the book and let's get shredding!

SUPERMAN SEATGRAB

TABLETOP

Chapter 6:
Dirt Riding

BMX FREESTYLE ISN'T JUST LIMITED TO SKATEPARKS AND streets, it also includes dirt riding. In this chapter, we'll take a look at the basics of dirt riding in BMX freestyle and some of the tricks and maneuvers that you can learn on them.

Dirt riding is a style of BMX freestyle that takes place on natural terrain such as dirt jumps, berms, and mounds. It's an exciting way to ride that offers a different set of challenges and obstacles than you would find in a Skatepark or on the streets.

To get started with dirt riding, you'll need a BMX bike with wider tires to handle the loose terrain. You'll also want to invest in some quality dirt riding gear, such as knee and elbow pads, and a full-face helmet. Safety is key when riding on natural terrain, and you'll want to make sure you're protected in case of a fall.

One of the basic tricks you'll want to learn when dirt riding is the table top. This trick involves riding up a dirt jump and jumping over the top, with both wheels of the bike off the ground. To perform a table top, you'll need to ride up to the jump at a moderate speed, pull up on the handlebars and use your legs and arms to bend the bike sideways to create style. Another popular trick in dirt riding is the moto-whip. This trick involves doing a 90-degree turn in the air while keeping the wheels level. To perform a moto-whip, you'll need to ride up to the jump, pull up on the handlebars, and use your body and handlebars to turn the bike.

The last basic trick you'll want to learn when dirt riding is the no-hand. This trick involves taking your hands off the bike while in the air. In order to perform the trick, you'll need to ride up to the jump, pull up on the handlebars and use your body and hands to tuck the bike's frame between your legs, gripping it with both of your knees. Once you've mastered this, you'll be able to take your hands off the handlebars. (Note: Be sure to put your hands back on the handlebars before landing to avoid any disastrous consequences).

MOTO-WHIP

DECADE

Dirt riding is a fun and challenging aspect of BMX freestyle that offers a different set of obstacles and challenges than you would find in a Skatepark or on the streets. With the right training, practice, and attitude, you'll be well on your way to mastering the art of dirt riding. Remember to always wear the proper safety gear, obey traffic laws and regulations, and have fun!

Yo! Just a quick heads up, that **BMX TRICK LIST** I made for you is waiting to be shredded! Packed with some seriously gnarly stunts, it's time to put your skills to the test. So, don't waste any more time, head to the back of the book and let's get riding like a boss!

FRONT YARD

Chapter 7:
Flatland BMX

ALRIGHT, NOW THAT WE'VE SHREDDED SOME DIRT JUMPS and been to the Skatepark, it's time to switch things up and check out a different BMX style. You ready for this? It's called Flatland and it's one of the most unique styles of BMX freestyle. Forget about bumps and jumps, flatland riding is all about smooth, flowy movements and technical tricks on a flat surface. It's time to show off your skills and step up your game.

In this chapter, we'll take a look at the basics of flatland riding and some of the tricks and maneuvers that you can learn. Flatland riding requires a different type of bike than the other styles of BMX freestyle, such as a flatland-specific bike, which has a shorter top tube and a steeper geometry, which allows the rider to help spin the bike around its own axis. You will also need a flat surface to practice on, such as a parking lot or a basketball court, where you can practice your moves.

One of the basic tricks you'll want to learn when flatland riding is the megaspin. This trick involves spinning the bike around its own axis while keeping one or both feet on the pegs (BMX pegs are those cylindrical metal attachments that stick out of the middle of your bike's wheels. They're like tiny platforms that you can stand on and perform all sorts of cool tricks like spins, grinds and stalls. Think of them as your secret weapon to BMX awesomeness! To perform a megaspin, you'll need to start by riding in a circle and gradually increasing your speed, then pull up on the handlebars and use your body and handlebars to spin around the backwheel with the bike.

Another popular trick in flatland riding is the steamroller. This trick involves standing of the pegs of the front wheel while riding backwords. To perform a steamroller, you'll need to grab the handlebar with one hand, then pull up on the seat with your other hand and lift up the back of the bike.

The last basic trick you'll want to learn when riding flatland is the Hang-5. This trick involves balancing on the front wheel of the bike while standing on the pegs and lifting the back wheel. To perform a Hang-5, you'll need to start by riding with a slow speed, then step on the front peg with one of your legs (keep your other leg in the air)

TIME-MACHINE

and balance the back wheel up in the air.

Flatland riding is a challenging and technical style of BMX freestyle that requires a lot of practice and patience. With the right training, practice, and attitude, you'll be well on your way to mastering the art of flatland riding.

HANG-5

Chapter 8:
Advanced BMX Tricks

As you progress in BMX freestyle, you'll want to learn more advanced tricks and maneuvers. In this chapter, we're diving into the ultimate moves like backflips, frontflips, decades and turndowns. These tricks will take your skills to the next level and make you look like a pro.

The backflip is the absolute BMX move, and it's where your wildest dreams come to life! Imagine soaring through the air, spinning around with your bike with effortless grace. But before you can master this epic trick, you'll need to hone your skills in the foam-pit. This is where you'll discover the true thrill of BMX riding, where you can push yourself to the limit without fear of injury. And the best part is, these foam-pits can be found in the most advanced indoor skateparks, where you'll join a community of like-minded riders, all pushing the boundaries of what's possible on two wheels. So what are you waiting for? It's time to experience the ultimate rush and make your BMX dreams a reality with the backflip!

To perform a backflip, you'll need to ride up to a

jump or ramp, pull up on the handlebars, and use your body to lean back, spinnin g around with the bike and landing back on your wheels once you completed the spin. Similarly, frontflips are the same only it requires pushing your body forwards to achieve the spin.

The decade is another advanced trick that involves spinning with the bike, but while only holding the handle-bars. To perform a decade you'll need to ride up to a jump or ramp, pull up on the handlebars, and use your legs to start a 360 jump around the bike, while holding the handle-bars. This trick requires a lot of strength and coordination, so it's important to start with small jumps and gradually work your way up to bigger jumps.

And now here's my personal favourite, the turn-down! The turndown is an advanced trick that involves riding up a ramp or quarter-pipe and then folding the bike in the air. To perform a turndown, you'll need to ride up to a ramp or quarter pipe, pull up on the handlebars, and once your high enough in the air, turn them backwards over your legs, so it looks like the bike is folded!

These tricks require a lot of practice and coordina-

INVERT

tion, so make sure you practice them it into a foam-pit first, then gradually work your way up to resi and normal ramps. You might wonder what's a resi? Resi-ramps have a layer of foam and a layer of plastic (made of resin, hence the name) that helps you to reduce your impact of landing for a safer way of practising!

BACKFLIP
X-UP

LAIDBACK
NOHANDER

FLAIR

Chapter 9:
Vert and Mega Ramps

ARE YOU READY FOR THE MOST DARING AND CHALLENG-
ing style yet? Vert ramp and mega ramp riding are two
advanced styles of BMX freestyle that take place on large
ramps with significant height. In this chapter, we'll take a
look at the basics of riding on vert ramps and mega ramps,
as well as some of the tricks and maneuvers that can be
performed on these types of ramps. Vert ramps are large
ramps that typically have a height of around 12-15 feet
and are used to perform tricks such as airs, grinds, and
spins. Vert riding requires a lot of speed and power, so it's
important to have a good level of physical fitness and to
practice regularly on smaller ramps before attempting to
ride on a vert ramp. Mega ramps are even larger ramps
that typically have a height of around 20-30 feet and are
used to perform tricks such as airs, spins, and combination tricks. Mega ramp riding requires a high level of skill
and experience, and is not recommended for beginners.
To ride on a vert ramp or mega ramp, it's important to
have the right equipment, such as a BMX bike with sturdy
wheels and a strong frame, as well as proper safety gear,

such as a full-face helmet, knee and elbow pads, and gloves. Some of the tricks that can be performed on vert ramps and mega ramps include the Superman Seat-Grab (yes you read that correctly) the 540 spin, and the Back-flip-Air otherwise known as the Flair. (Wow, these are the tricks that you really should check out on your **BMX TRICK LIST!**) And we can't forget about Big-Air jumps either! Big-Air is a style where the rider jumps high into the air on a vert or mega ramp and performs various tricks such as spins or flips but mostly aiming for height. Big-air jumps are one of the most exciting and thrilling aspects of BMX freestyle riding. To perform a big-air jump, the rider will start by approaching the ramp at a high speed and then use the ramp's transition to jump into the air. The rider will then use the momentum to perform a trick while in the air.

Big-air jumps can be challenging and require a lot of practice and skill to master, but they are also very re-warding when executed correctly. It's important to always wear proper protective gear, such as a helmet and pads, and to practice in a safe and controlled environment. It's also very important to be familiar with the ramp and its characteristics before attempting any big-air jumps.

SUPERMAN

360 SPIN

Chapter 10:
The Competition

LET'S DO THIS! IT'S TIME TO SHOW OFF ALL THE SKILLS you've learned and dominate at your first BMX freestyle competition!

As you progress, you may be interested in competing in BMX freestyle competitions. In this chapter, we'll take a look at the aspects of competition in BMX freestyle, including what to expect, how to prepare, and how to stay safe.

BMX freestyle competitions are organized events that showcase the skills of BMX riders. They usually take place at Skateparks or other venues and are typically organized by local BMX clubs or organizations. There are different types of competitions, including jam sessions, where riders take turns performing tricks, and timed runs, where riders perform a set of tricks within a certain amount of time.

To prepare for a BMX freestyle competition, it's important to practice your tricks and maneuvers regularly. It's also important to stay in good physical shape, as BMX freestyle is a demanding sport that requires a lot of strength and endurance.

When competing in a BMX freestyle competition, it's important to wear the proper safety gear, such as a helmet, gloves, knee and elbow pads, and proper shoes. It's also important to be respectful of the area and the people around you. Remember, when you're at competitions, you never know who might be watching. It's important to always give it your best, because you never know when a sponsor might take notice of your skills and offer you an opportunity to ride professionally. So, keep riding, keep pushing yourself and stay focused, you never know what opportunities can come from a competition.

BMX freestyle competitions can be a great way to showcase your skills and meet other riders. They are a fun and exciting way to take your riding to the next level, but it's important to remember that safety always comes first. So, grab your bike and get out there and ride, and have fun competing!

BACKFLIP

SET THE TRICK

Chapter 11:
Game of B.I.K.E.

On a sunny afternoon at the skatepark, you and your BMX crew are in search of a fresh challenge. That's when someone proposes the ultimate BMX showdown: Game of B.I.K.E. It's a thrilling and entertaining game that will not only test your BMX skills but also bring laughter and cheers from everyone.

Getting Started

1. Choose the First Rider: To kick things off, determine who goes first. This can be settled with a game of rock, paper, scissors, or any other method you prefer.

2. Set the Opening Trick: The rider who starts has the honor of setting the initial trick. It can be a stylish jump, a slick grind, or a unique trick. Let your creativity shine and demonstrate your skills, but make sure it's a trick you can confidently execute.

3. Attempt to Match It: Once the opening trick is set, the other participants have three tries to replicate it. This is where the challenge begins. Strive to mimic the trick exactly as it was performed.

4. Avoid Collecting Letters: Here's the catch: If you can't execute the trick after three attempts, you earn the first letter, 'B.' Be cautious, as accumulating letters will bring you closer to being out of the game.

Winning the Game

The game progresses as each player takes turns setting tricks and attempting to match them. As the tricks become more daring, the excitement level soars. The last rider standing without spelling out B.I.K.E. emerges as the champion and earns the prestigious title of the champion.

3 ATTEMPTS TO LAND IT

TAILWHIP

Game Of B.I.K.E.
Tips

1. Unleash Your Creativity: When setting a trick, let your imagination run wild, but keep in mind the skill levels of your fellow BMX riders. Strive for a balance between challenge and fairness.

2. Embrace the Spectators: Even if you're no longer in the game, relish the opportunity to cheer on your friends and witness their incredible tricks.

3. Practice Makes Perfect: Game of B.I.K.E. is an excellent way to hone your skills. The more you practice, the more proficient you'll become.

4. Friendly Rivalry: Remember, it's all in the spirit of fun. Applaud your friends and don't hesitate to share a laugh at your own attempts. The aim is to revel in the game, enhance your skills, and strengthen friendships.

Game of B.I.K.E. is not merely a showcase of your BMX talents; it's a chance to connect with your friends, display your tricks, and craft enduring memories at the skatepark. So, the next time you're there, don't miss the opportunity to challenge your buddies to a round of Game of B.I.K.E. and discover who will emerge as the BMX master!

DON'T FORGET
YOUR HELMET

Wrapping up

IN THIS BOOK, WE'VE EXPLORED THE EXCITING WORLD OF BMX freestyle, from the basics of riding to advanced tricks and competition. Who knows, perhaps one day the Olympic dream might come knocking on your door. It's important to remember that becoming a professional BMX freestyle rider and competing in the Olympics takes dedication, hard work, and a passion for the sport.

Always wear proper safety gear, practice in a safe and controlled environment, and never attempt tricks that are above your skill level. But most importantly, always have fun!

Remember to keep pushing yourself, keep learning and keep riding. Who knows, one day you might be standing on the podium at the Olympic Games, with a medal around your neck, all because you fell in love with the thrill of BMX freestyle. Believe in your potential, stay dedicated, and never stop pursuing your passion for BMX freestyle. With each ride, every new trick you master, and every competition you conquer, you're writing your own story in the world of extreme sports.

Becoming a pro at BMX freestyle riding is an exhilarating journey. To maximize your progress, follow these key steps:

1. Master Your Trick List: Treat your Trick List as your roadmap to conquering awesome tricks that will set you apart.

2. Utilize Your 'My Tricklist' Journal: Keep a record of your tricks, monitor your progress, and set fresh goals in your journal.

3. Maintain Your BMX: Regular bike maintenance ensures your BMX is always in peak condition for your next ride.

4. Unleash Your Creativity with the BMX designer: Personalize your BMX's colors and design to make it uniquely yours.

5. Challenge Friends with Game of B.I.K.E.: Engage in friendly competitions with your fellow riders, pushing each other to new heights.

6. Stay Organized for Competitions: Utilize the Competition Journal to document your accomplishments and experiences on your journey.

Armed with these strategies, you're on your way to BMX freestyle excellence. Keep riding, savor every moment, and stay fearless. More epic BMX adventures await in the Rider Team series. It's been a pleasure guiding you. Happy BMX freestyling!

That's a wrap! Enjoyed the ride with Matt from the Rider Team? Keep practicing those tricks, and if you're hungry for more action, watch for the next books in the series. See you at the skatepark!

KEEP SHREDDING!

BMX TRICKLIST

A COOL STICKER TO BE PLACED NEXT TO EACH TRICK ONCE IT'S learned (purchased from your local bike shop) or just simply ticked out with a pen or pencil.

BASIC TRICKS

1. Basic Stance: Stand over your bike with one foot on each pedal and have the cranks level. Keep your knees slightly bent, and your arms should be relaxed with your hands on the handlebars.

2. Bunny Hop: A basic jump where the rider lifts the front and rear wheel of the bike off the ground, first the front-wheel then the back-wheel.

3. Manual: A trick where the rider balances on the rear wheel while riding forward.

SKATEPARK TRICKS

4. 360 Spins: A trick where the rider performs a bunny-hop and spins with the bike 360 degrees. ☐

5. Barspin: A trick where the rider spins the handlebars 360 degrees while keeping the rest of the bike stationary. ☐

6. Tailwhip: A trick where the rider spins the bike 360 degrees while holding nothing but the handlebars. ☐

DIRT TRICKS

7. Tabletop: Ride up to the jump at a moderate speed, pull up on the handlebars and use your legs and arms to bend the bike sideways to create style. ☐

8. Moto-whip: To perform a moto-whip, you'll need to ride up to the jump, pull up on the handlebars, and use your body and handlebars to turn the bike 90 degrees in the air. ☐

9.No-hand: This trick involves taking your hands off the bike whilst being in the air. There are multiple variations of this trick. ☐

FLATLAND TRICKS

9. Megaspin: To perform a megaspin, you'll need to start by riding in a circle and gradually increasing your speed, then pull up on the handlebars and use your body and handlebars to spin around the backwheel with the bike.

☐

10. Steamroller: This trick involves standing on the pegs of the front wheel while riding backwords. To perform a steamroller, you'll need to grab the handlebar with one hand, then pull up on the seat with your other hand and lift up the back of the bike.

☐

11. Hang-5: Start by riding with a slow speed, then step on the front peg with one of your legs (keep your other leg in the air) and balance the back wheel up in the air while riding along.

☐

PRO TRICKS

12.Backflips and Frontflips: To perform a backflip, you'll need to ride up to a jump or ramp, pull up on the handlebars, and use your body to lean back, spinnig around with the bike and landing back on your wheels once you completed the spin. Similarly, frontflips are the same only it requires pushing your body forwards to achieve the spin.

13.Decade: To perform a decade you'll need to ride up to a jump or ramp, pull up on the handlebars, and use your legs to start a 360 jump around the bike, while holding the handlebars.

14. Turn Down: To perform a turndown, you'll need to ride up to a ramp or quarter pipe, pull up on the handlebars, and once your high enough in the air, turn them backwards over your legs, so it looks like the bike is folded!

PRO TRICKS

15. Superman-seatgrab: You might want to look this one up. To perform this trick start by riding up to a jump and as you're leaving the lip, pull up on the handlebars and simultaneously kick your legs backwards, meanwhile reach back and grab the seat with one hand and super-extend the bike in front of you. Once you've got a good grip on the seat, tuck in your legs and prepare for landing.

16. 540 Spin: To do a 540, ride up to a ramp or quarter-pipe. While in the air, spin with your bike 360 degrees and then another 180 degrees. This trick can be multiplied, like the 900 spin.

Note: These electrifying tricks are depicted with illustrations in the book, providing a visual guide to mastering each technique. For example, Trick Number 15 is on the back cover! Can you find them all?

17. Flair (Aka Flip-air): You also might want to look this one up. Also probably watch some videos of it. The Flair trick involves doing a Backflip while turning around on a quater-pipe, with an additional 180 degrees rotation, creating one of the most spectacular tricks out there. To execute this trick you need to have a good understanding of backflips and spins, and make sure to practice it into a foam pit before attempting it on wooden or metal ramps.

Note: BMX freestyle is a creative sport, you don't have to stick to a certain style of riding, you can try out
different tricks and find your own unique style.
As you continue to ride and learn new tricks, you'll be able to evolve and develop your own personal style. It's all about having fun, experimenting and pushing the limits. However It's always recommended to seek instruction from certified BMX coaches and to wear proper protective gear while practicing.

MY TRICKLIST JOURNAL

INTRODUCING THE ULTIMATE TRICKLIST JOURNAL, DESIGNED to help you track and perfect your BMX tricks. As you progress simply add new tricks to your journal, which will serve as a reminder of what you've learned, and what you still need to work on.

☐

☐

☐

☐

☐

MY TRICKLIST JOURNAL

☐

☐

☐

☐

☐

☐

MY TRICKLIST JOURNAL

☐

☐

☐

☐

☐

☐

MY TRICKLIST JOURNAL

☐

☐

☐

☐

☐

☐

MY TRICKLIST JOURNAL

☐

☐

☐

☐

☐

☐

MY TRICKLIST JOURNAL

☐

☐

☐

☐

☐

☐

BMX DESIGNER

BIKE CHECK

Frame:

Forks:

Handlebars:

Stem:

Grips:

Brakes:

Seat:

Seatpost:

Pedals:

Cranks:

Sprocket:

Chain:

Tyres:

Rims:

Front Hub:

Spokes:

Rear Hub:

BMX DESIGNER

BIKE CHECK

Frame:

Forks:

Handlebars:

Stem:

Grips:

Brakes:

Seat:

Seatpost:

Pedals:

Cranks:

Sprocket:

Chain:

Tyres:

Rims:

Front Hub:

Spokes:

Rear Hub:

BMX DESIGNER

BIKE CHECK

Frame:

Forks:

Handlebars:

Stem:

Grips:

Brakes:

Seat:

Seatpost:

Pedals:

Cranks:

Sprocket:

Chain:

Tyres:

Rims:

Front Hub:

Spokes:

Rear Hub:

BMX DESIGNER

BIKE CHECK

Frame:

Forks:

Handlebars:

Stem:

Grips:

Brakes:

Seat:

Seatpost:

Pedals:

Cranks:

Sprocket:

Chain:

Tyres:

Rims:

Front Hub:

Spokes:

Rear Hub:

BMX DESIGNER

BIKE CHECK

Frame:

Forks:

Handlebars:

Stem:

Grips:

Brakes:

Seat:

Seatpost:

Pedals:

Cranks:

Sprocket:

Chain:

Tyres:

Rims:

Front Hub:

Spokes:

Rear Hub:

MY COMPETITIONS AND ACHIEVEMENTS

THE COMPETITION JOURNAL IS AN ESSENTIAL TOOL FOR BMX riders competing at any level. Use it to track progress, document runs, and stay positive as you prepare for competitions. A reminder to stay focused and there's always an opportunity to learn and grow.

Competition Entered:
Location:
Date:
Category:
Placement:
How was it:

Competition Entered:
Location:
Date:
Category:
Placement:
How was it:

Competition Entered:
Location:
Date:
Category:
Placement:
How was it:

Competition Entered:
Location:
Date:
Category:
Placement:
How was it:

Competition Entered:
Location:
Date:
Category:
Placement:
How was it:

Competition Entered:
Location:
Date:
Category:
Placement:
How was it:

Competition Entered:
Location:
Date:
Category:
Placement:
How was it:

Competition Entered:
Location:
Date:
Category:
Placement:
How was it:

Competition Entered:
Location:
Date:
Category:
Placement:
How was it:

Competition Entered:
Location:
Date:
Category:
Placement:
How was it:

Competition Entered:
Location:
Date:
Category:
Placement:
How was it:

Competition Entered:
Location:
Date:
Category:
Placement:
How was it:

Competition Entered:
Location:
Date:
Category:
Placement:
How was it:

Competition Entered:
Location:
Date:
Category:
Placement:
How was it:

Competition Entered:
Location:
Date:
Category:
Placement:
How was it:

DON'T MISS THE NEXT
BOOKS IN THE SERIES

INTERACTIVE

SCOOTERING
UNLEASHED

A BEGINNER'S GUIDE TO EXTREME SCOOTERING

BEN RIDER

DON'T MISS THE NEXT BOOKS IN THE SERIES

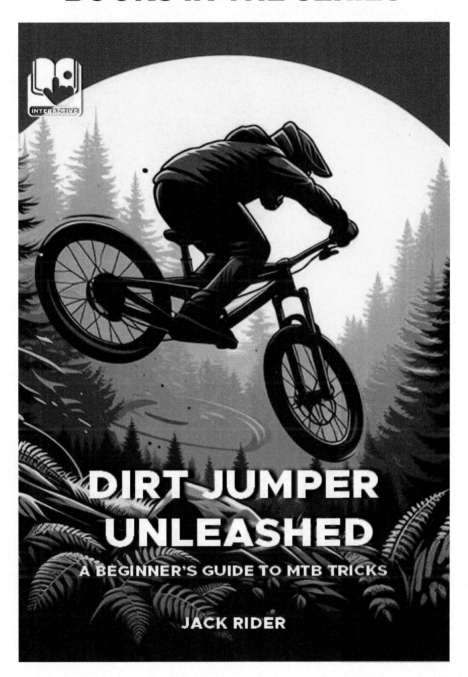

DIRT JUMPER UNLEASHED

A BEGINNER'S GUIDE TO MTB TRICKS

JACK RIDER

DON'T MISS THE NEXT BOOKS IN THE SERIES

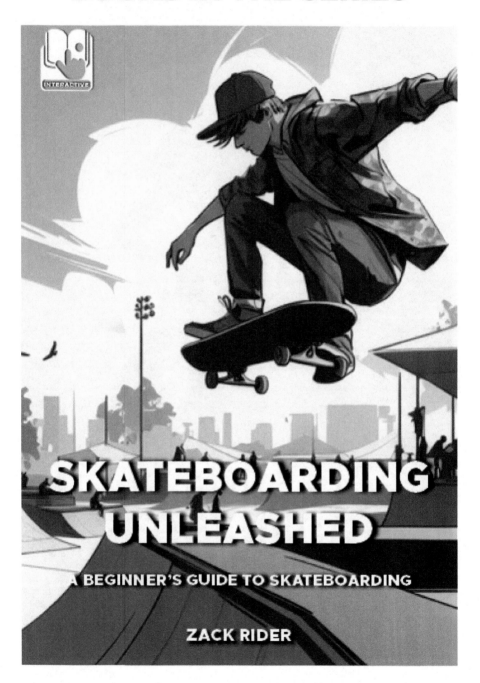

SKATEBOARDING UNLEASHED

A BEGINNER'S GUIDE TO SKATEBOARDING

ZACK RIDER

Thank you for embarking on an adventure with the Rider Team Adventures Book Series! If you enjoyed the journey, please consider leaving a review on your purchase platform to help others discover and share the joy of outdoor and extreme sports. Join the movement by keeping an eye out for newcomers wherever you go—whether it's the skatepark, streets, slopes, waves, or any other action-packed terrain. Your support helps us inspire enthusiasts across all sports. Happy riding, skating, and shredding, no matter your chosen discipline!

Printed in Great Britain
by Amazon